0.5

D0866869

A NOTE TO PARENTS

Reading Aloud with Your Child
Research shows that reading books aloud is the single most valuable support parents can provide in helping children learn to read.
- Be a ham! The more enthusiasm you display, the more your child will enjoy the book.
- Run your finger underneath the words as you read to signal that the print carries the story.
- Leave time for examining the illustrations more closely; encourage your child to find things in the pictures.
- Invite your youngster to join in whenever there's a repeated phrase in the text.
- Link up events in the book with similar events in your child's life.
- If your child asks a question, stop and answer it. The book can be a means to learning more about your child's thoughts.

Listening to Your Child Read Aloud
The support of your attention and praise is absolutely crucial to your child's continuing efforts to learn to read.
- If your child is learning to read and asks for a word, give it immediately so that the meaning of the story is not interrupted. DO NOT ask your child to sound out the word.
- On the other hand, if your child initiates the act of sounding out, don't intervene.
- If your child is reading along and makes what is called a miscue, listen for the sense of the miscue. If the word "road" is substituted for the word "street," for instance, no meaning is lost. Don't stop the reading for a correction.
- If the miscue makes no sense (for example, "horse" for "house"), ask your child to reread the sentence because you're not sure you understand what's just been read.
- Above all else, enjoy your child's growing command of print and make sure you give lots of praise. *You are your child's first teacher — and the most important one. Praise from you is critical for further risk-taking and learning.*

— Priscilla Lynch
Ph.D., New York University
Educational Consultant

To friends of whales everywhere
— F.M.

For my dad with all my love
— L.S.

Text copyright © 1996 by Faith McNulty.
Illustrations copyright © 1996 by Lena Shiffman.
All rights reserved. Published by Scholastic Inc.
HELLO READER!, CARTWHEEL BOOKS, and the CARTWHEEL BOOKS
logo are registered trademarks of Scholastic Inc.

Library of Congress Cataloging-in-Publication Data

McNulty, Faith
    Listening to Whales Sing / by Faith McNulty ; illustrated by Lena Shiffman.
       p.   cm. — (Hello reader! Level 4)
    Summary: While observing whales in the Atlantic Ocean, a girl falls overboard.
    ISBN 0-590-47871-0
    [1. Whales — Fiction.] I. Shiffman, Lena, ill. II. Title.   III. Series.
PZ7.M24Li 1995
[Fic] — dc20

94-40993
CIP
AC

12 11 10 9 8 7 6 5 4 3 2 1   6 7 8 9/9 0 1/0

Printed in the U.S.A.   23

First Scholastic printing, April 1996

Listening to
Whales Sing

by Faith McNulty

Illustrated by Lena Shiffman

Hello Reader! — Level 4

SCHOLASTIC INC. **Cartwheel**
·B·O·O·K·S· ®

New York Toronto London Auckland Sydney

I was very lucky once.
I heard whales singing.
This is what I remember.

I am in a small boat
that rocks on the waves
far from shore
in the Atlantic Ocean.
Somewhere in the deep,
dark water below are whales.
Huge, mysterious creatures
glide through the watery world
that is their home.
I can't see the whales,
but I can hear them.

Strange sounds are being picked up
by a microphone
that we have dropped
into the deep water below us.
A cord, hundreds of feet long,
connects it to our headphones.
Listening, I hear weird music
or something
that sounds
like music—

brassy trumpets, sweet violins,
deep, throaty horns—
as though an orchestra is tuning up
at the bottom of the sea.
Then come high, silvery voices
singing a beautiful song.
I imagine fairies of the deep
dancing amidst seaweed and coral.

I shiver with excitement
and look at my friend Kevin.
He is listening, too,
on another set of headphones,
and smiling.
He is a scientist who studies whales,
especially the sounds that whales make.
He hopes, someday,
to understand their meaning.

Are the whales talking
to one another?
Are they singing love songs
as they search for a mate?
Or just keeping in touch
with other whales
over the vast distances
of the sea?
It is a puzzle
no one has solved.

Suddenly the song ends.
We take off our headphones and relax.
Jenny, Kevin's wife and partner in research,
passes out cheese and crackers.
While we eat, we watch the sea
for the sight of a whale
coming up to breathe.

Whales are not fish.
They breathe air through nostrils
called blowholes
placed at the top of their heads.
A whale can take a breath
without raising its head
more than a few inches above water.
When the whale dives underwater
the blowholes close.
But every five or ten minutes
the whale comes to the surface
to take a breath.

It blows stale air
out of its lungs
in a steamy spout,
then takes a fresh breath
and dives again.

The spout can be seen
for a mile or so.
And that is how whale hunters
find their prey.
In the past hundred years,
whalers have killed so many
of the largest whales
that only a few of the giants
remain alive to carry on their species.

Kevin and Jenny hope that their research will teach people that no more whales should be hunted and killed.

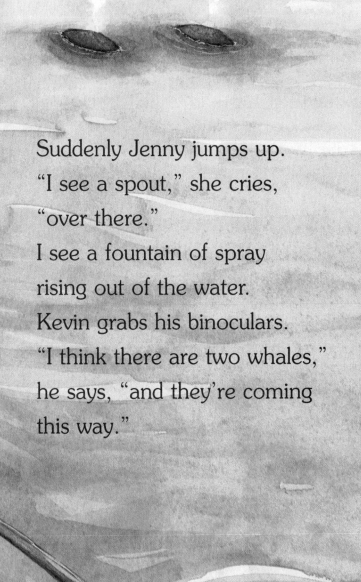

Suddenly Jenny jumps up.
"I see a spout," she cries,
"over there."
I see a fountain of spray
rising out of the water.
Kevin grabs his binoculars.
"I think there are two whales,"
he says, "and they're coming
this way."

He quickly decides
he will try to photograph them
from the little rowboat
that we tow behind us.
He zips on a wet suit,
hauls the boat alongside,
and jumps in.
"Me too!" I call
and jump in
after him.

The little boat rocks
on the waves.
It seems very small.
The surface of the surging,
foaming, green water
is very close.
I feel the power
of the ocean swells
that lift and drop our little boat
as though it were a bathtub toy.

Kevin, camera in hand,
stands on the seat beside me,
swaying to the motion of the waves.
We wait—tense and excited.
Will the whales come closer?
Or will they dive and disappear?
Minutes pass.
No whales.
Nothing but endless waves.
They foam and surge
as far as we can see.

Then, suddenly,
only a few hundred yards away,
a huge, dark form shoots out
of the water.
For an instant,
it seems to hang in the air,
then falls flat
with a giant splash.
It is a breaching whale.

It sinks out of sight,
but another whale spouts,
even closer.
I glimpse its dark, rounded back,
gleaming like a wet inner tube,
before it disappears.

"I'm going to try
for an underwater shot,"
Kevin yells,
and leaps into the water.

I am alone in the rocking boat.
Again the whales have disappeared
beneath the surface. Are they coming closer?
Or have they dived into the depths?
To see better I stand up
on the seat.
Watching the glassy green water
swirl and heave,
I picture the whales
gliding through the
darkness below me
like living submarines.

Suddenly it happens.
Almost beside me — a whale
comes up and spouts.

I can see the blowhole
on the top of its head;
it opens as the whale
breathes out — then in.
I can see its long, dark back
and a flipper, shaped like
the wing of an airplane.

I even think I glimpse an eye looking
right at me. My heart almost stops.
As the whale dives down again,
giant flukes rise from the water.
They look like the wings
of a huge butterfly.

The whale disappears.
The little boat rocks—
I lose my balance
and fall into cold, cold water.
I come up splashing and fighting
to get my breath.
I hear Jenny yelling for Kevin.
She is standing up in the boat, waving.
She throws a life ring into the water,
but it lands far away—out of my reach.

"Take it easy!" she calls.
"Don't panic! We'll get you!"
Her voice reminds me
of my water-safety lessons.
The first rule is to stop struggling.
I make myself calm down,
relax, and float.
Then I swim slowly
toward the life ring.
I reach it and hold on.
A moment later Kevin is beside me.
He tows me to the little boat
and helps me climb in.
Nearby, a circle of slick, swirling water
marks the spot where the whales
dove down into the deep.

Later, back aboard the big boat
I am in dry clothes
and drinking hot tea.
I am ashamed,
but Kevin and Jenny are kind.
They praise my swimming
and don't say I was a fool
to fall in.
They are thrilled
that the whales came so close
and that Kevin was able
to photograph them.
After a while,
when we have settled down,
Jenny and Kevin begin again,
to watch and listen for whales.

Jenny hands me a pair of headphones.
I put them on.
There are no whales in sight.

The sea looks empty.
But listening, I hear whale sounds,
faint at first, then louder,
coming out of the deep.
It is a thrilling sound.
I feel as though
the whales are telling me something
that I cannot put into words.
I look at Jenny.
"I wish I knew what they are saying,"
I tell her.
She nods and answers,
"Yes, me too."

"Maybe they are saying something like this:
'We whales are one of the greatest wonders
of the earth. We are part of the great chain
that links all living things. We harm no one.
Please let us live our lives peacefully,
unharmed by humans.'"

I nod yes.
Jenny and I smile because
we share the same feelings.

This adventure was quite a while ago,
but I have never forgotten a moment of it,
or the message from the whales.